BLACK BEAUTY

BY ANNA SEWELL

Retold by Quinn Currie

Illustrated by Donna Ryan

Storytellers Ink

Seattle, Washington

ISBN 0-9623072-2-X

Printed in the United States of America

Dedicated to Cleveland Amory

This centennial edition of Black Beauty is dedicated to a young man from Boston, who like countless other children read and loved the story of this fine horse.

Black Beauty's touching words in the closing lines of his story moved this young man to vow one day to provide such a place for other animals in need:

> "I have nothing to fear; And here my story ends.
>   My troubles are all over, and I am at home."

Now these famous words hang over the entrance to the Black Beauty Ranch in Murchison, Texas, which he founded.

His illustrious life and literary brilliance have glittered with the best of them, but his love of the defenseless is what shines through, as he's grown from Cleveland, the boy, into Amory, the man.

CONTENTS

Chapter I
MY EARLY HOME

The first place that I can remember was a large pleasant meadow with a pond of clear water in it. Shady trees leaned over the pond, and rushes and water lilies grew at the deep end. Over the hedge on one side we looked into a plowed field, and on the other we looked over a gate at our master's house, which stood by the roadside. At the top of the meadow was a plantation of fir trees, and at the bottom a running brook overhung by a steep bank.

While I was young I lived on my mother's milk, as I could not yet eat grass. In the daytime I ran by her side, and at night I lay down close beside her. When it was hot, we used to stand by the pond in the shade of the trees, and when it was cold, we had a nice warm shed near the plantation.

As soon as I was old enough to eat grass, my mother would go out to work in the daytime, and come back in the evening.

There were six young colts in the meadow with me. They were older than I was; some were nearly as large as grown-up horses. I used to run with them, and had great fun; we used to gallop together all around the field as hard as we could go. Sometimes we played rather rough, for they frequently bit and kicked as they galloped.

One day, when there was a good deal of kicking, my mother whinnied to me to come to her, and said:

"I want you to pay attention to what I am going to say to you. The colts who live here are very good colts, but they are cart-horse colts, and they have not learned manners. You have been well bred. Your father has a great name in these parts, and your grandfather won the cup two years at the Newmarket races; your grandmother had the sweetest temper of any horse I ever knew, and I don't think you have ever seen me kick or bite. I hope you will grow up gentle and good, and never learn bad ways. Do your work with a good will, lift your feet up well when you trot, and never bite or kick, even in play."

I have not forgotton my mother's advice. I knew she was a wise horse, and our master thought a great deal of her. Her name was Dutchess, but he often called her Pet.

Our master was a good, kind man. He gave us good food, good lodging, and kind words. He spoke as kindly to us as he did to his little children. We were all fond of him, and my mother loved him very much. When she saw him at the gate, she would neigh with joy, and trot up to him. He would pat and stroke her and say, "Hello Pet, and how is your little Darkie?" I was a dull black, so he called me Darkie; then he would give me a piece of bread, which was very good, and sometimes he brought a carrot for my mother. All the horses would come to him, but I think we were his favorites. My mother always took him to town on market day in a light cart.

There was a plowboy, Dick, who sometimes came into our field to pluck blackberries from the hedge. When he had eaten all he wanted, he would have what he called fun with the colts, throwing stones and sticks at them to make them gallop. We did not much mind him, for we could gallop off; but sometimes a stone would hit and hurt us.

One day he was at this game, and did not know that the master was in the next field watching what was going on. The master jumped over the hedge, and caught Dick by the arm so suddenly that he roared with surprise. As soon as we saw the master, we trotted up nearer to see what was going on.

"Wretched boy!" he said.   "The colts feel pain just as much as you do. This is not the first time, nor the second that you have tormented them, but it shall be the last.   There - take your money and go home.   I do not want to see you on my farm again."   And we never did see Dick again.   Daniel, the man who looked after all the horses, was just as gentle as our master, so we were very happy under his care.

Chapter II
MY BREAKING IN

I was now beginning to grow up. My coat had grown fine and soft, and was bright black. I had one white foot, and a white star on my forehead. I was thought to be very handsome. My master decided not to sell me till I was four years old. He said boys should not work like men, and colts should not work like horses, until they were quite grown up.

When I was four years old, Squire Gordon came to look at me. He examined my eyes, my mouth, and my legs. He felt them all down, and then I had to walk, trot and gallop before him. He seemed to like me, and said, "When he has been well broken in, he will do very well." My master said he would break me in himself, as he should not like me to be frightened or hurt; and he lost no time about it, for the next day he began.

Everyone may not know what breaking in is, therefore I will describe it. It means to teach a horse to wear a saddle and bridle and to carry on his back a man, woman, or child; and to respond to the riders directions quickly and gently. The horse must also learn to wear a collar, and a breeching, and to stand still while they are put on; then to have a cart or a carriage fixed behind him, so that he cannot walk or trot without dragging it after him; and he must go fast or slow, just as his driver wishes. He must never jerk at what he sees, nor speak to other horses, nor bite, nor kick, nor have any will of his own; but always do his master's will, even though he may be very tired or hungry. But worst of all, once his harness is on, he may neither jump for joy nor lie down for weariness. So you can imagine how hard this breaking in is for a young and spirited animal.

I had of course been used to a halter, and to be led about in the field and lanes quietly, but now I was to have a bit and a bridle. My master gave me some oats as usual, and after a good deal of coaxing, he got the bit into my mouth, and the bridle fixed. Those who have never had a bit in their mouths can't imagine how bad it feels. A piece of cold hard steel as thick as a man's finger is pushed into your mouth, between your teeth and over your tongue, with the ends coming out at the corners of your mouth, and held fast there by straps over your head, under your throat, round your nose, and under your chin; so that in no way can you get rid of the nasty hard thing. It is very bad! At least I thought so. But I knew my mother always wore one when she went out, and all horses did when they were grown up, so with the nice oats, and my master's pats, kind words, and gentle ways, I slowly learned to wear my bit and bridle.

Next came the saddle, which was not half so bad. My master put it on my back very gently, while Daniel held my head; then he fastened the girths under my body, patting and talking to me all the time. Then I had a few oats, and was lead around a little. He did this every day till I began to look for the oats and the saddle. One morning my master got on my back and rode me around the meadow on the soft grass. It felt very strange; but I must say I was also rather proud to carry my master, and as he continued to ride me a little every day I soon became accustomed to it.

The next unpleasant business was putting on the iron shoes. That too was very hard at first. My master went with me to the blacksmith's forge, to see that I was not hurt or frightened. The blacksmith took my feet in his hand one after the other, and cut away some of the hoof. It did not cause pain, so I stood quietly until he had done them all. Then he took a piece of iron the shape of my foot, clapped it on, and drove some nails through the shoe into my hoof, so that the shoe was firmly on. My feet felt very stiff and heavy, but in time I got used to it.

With all this accomplished, my master then began to break me to harness. There were more new things to wear. First, a stiff heavy collar on my neck, and a bridle with great side-pieces against my eyes called blinkers, and blinkers indeed they were, for I could not see on either side, but only straight in front of me. However, in time I got used to everything, and could do my work as well as my mother.

I want to mention one part of my training, which I have always considered a great advantage. My master sent me for a fortnight to a neighboring farm which had a meadow that was skirted on one side by the railroad. Here some sheep and cows were grazing, and I was turned in among them.

I shall never forget the first train that passed by the meadow. I was feeding quietly near the fence which separated it from the railway, when I heard a strange sound in the distance, and before I knew it - with a rush and a clatter and a great puffing of smoke - a long black train thundered by, and was gone almost before I could draw my breath. I turned and galloped to the far side of the meadow as fast as I could, and stood there snorting with astonishment and fear.

In the course of the day many trains came by, some more slowly. These drew up at the station close by, sometimes with awful shrieks and groans. I thought it very dreadful, but the cows went on eating, and hardly raised their heads as the great, frightful things came puffing and grinding past.

For the first few days I could not feed in peace; but when I found out that this terrible creature never came into the field, or did me any harm, I began to disregard it, and very soon I cared as little about the passing of a train as the cows and sheep did.

My master often drove me in double harness with my mother because she was steady, and could teach me better than a strange horse could. She told me the better I behaved, the better I would be treated, and that it is always wisest to do my best to please my master. "But," said she, "there are a great many kinds of men. There are good, thoughtful men like our master that any horse would be proud to serve; and there are bad, cruel men, who never should have a horse or dog to call their own. Besides, there are a great many foolish men, ignorant and careless, who never trouble themselves to think. I hope you will fall into good hands, but a horse never knows who may buy him. It's all a chance for us, but do your best wherever it is, and keep up your good name."

Chapter III
BIRTWICK PARK

Early in May of that year there came a man from Squire Gordon's, who took me away to Birtwick Park. My master said, "Good-bye, Darkie. Be a good horse, and always do your best." I could not say good-bye, so I put my nose into his hand. He patted me kindly, and I left my first home.

Squire Gordon's Park skirted the village of Birtwick. It was entered by a large iron gate, and then you trotted along on a smooth road between clumps of large old trees; then through another gate, which brought you to the Hall, and beyond this lay the home paddock, the old orchard, and the stables. There was accommodation for many horses and carriages, and the stable into which I was taken was very roomy, with four good stalls and a large swinging window opening into the yard, which made it pleasant and airy.

The first stall was a large one with a wooden gate. The others were good stalls, but not as large. It had a low rack for hay and a low manger for corn.

It was called a loose box, because the horse put into it was not tied up, but left loose. It is a great thing to have a loose box.

Into this fine box the groom put me; it was clean, sweet, and airy, and the sides were not too high so that I could see all that went on. The groom

11

gave me some oats, patted me, spoke kindly to me, and then went away.

When I had eaten I looked around. In the stall next to mine stood a little fat pony, with a thick mane and tail, a very pretty head, and a pert little nose.

I put my head at the iron rails on top of my box and said, "How do you do?"

He turned around, held up his head, and said, "My name is Merrylegs. I carry the family on my back. They think a great deal of me, and so does James, the stable boy. Are you going to live next door to me here?"

"Yes," I said.

"Well, then," he said, "I hope you are good-tempered; I don't like anyone next door who bites."

Just then a horse's head appeared from the stall beyond; with eyes that looked rather ill-tempered. This was a tall chestnut mare, with a long handsome neck. She looked across to me and said:

"So it is you, a colt, who have turned me out of my home."

"I have turned no one out," I said. "The man who brought me put me here, and I had nothing to do with it. As for being a colt, I am four years old and a full grown horse."

In the afternoon when she went out, Merrylegs told me her story.

"Ginger has a bad habit of biting and snapping," said Merrylegs. "That is why they call her Ginger. When she was in the loose box she used to snap a lot. One day she bit James in the arm, and so the children, Flora and Jessie, were afraid to come into the stable. They are very fond of me, and used to bring me nice things to eat, an apple, or carrot, or piece of bread; but after Ginger arrived in that box they dared not come, and I miss them very much. I hope you don't bite or snap, so they will come again."

I told him I never bit anything but grass, oats, and corn, and could not think what pleasure Ginger found in it.

"Well, I don't think she finds pleasure," said Merrylegs. "It's just a bad habit. She says no one was ever kind to her, so why shouldn't she snap? If all she says is true, she must have been very abused before she came here. James does all he can to please her, and our master would never use a whip on a well-behaved horse. You see, I am twelve years old; I know a great deal, and I can tell you there is no better place for a horse than this. So it's Ginger's own fault that she wasn't allowed to stay in that box."

Chapter IV
A FAIR START

The next morning, John Manly, our coachman, took me into the yard and gave me a good grooming. Just as I was going into my box, with my coat soft and bright, the Squire came in to look at me. He seemed very pleased.

"John," he said, "you may as well take him around after breakfast."

"I will, sir," said John. After breakfast he came and fitted me with a bridle and saddle. He rode me slowly at first, then at a trot, then a canter, and when we were on the common we had a spendid gallop.

"Ho! ho, my boy," he said, as he pulled me up, "you would like to follow the hounds, I think."

As we came back through the Park we met the Squire and Mrs. Gordon walking; they stopped, and John jumped off.

"Well, John, how does he go?"

"First rate, sir," answered John, "he is as fleet as a deer, and has a fine spirit too; but the lightest touch of the rein will guide him. Down at the end of the common we met one of those traveling merchandise carts, hung all over with pots, pans, rugs, and the like. You know, sir, many horses will not pass those carts quietly; he just took a good look at it, and then went on as quiet and pleasant as could be. They were shooting rabbits near the Highwood, and a gun went off close by. He pulled up a little and looked, but did not stir a step to the right or left. I just held the rein steady and did not hurry him, and it's my opinion he has not been frightened or ill-used while he was young."

"That's good," said the Squire, "I will try him myself tomorrow."

The next day I was brought to my master. I remembered my mother's counsel, and I tried to do exactly what he wanted me to do. I found he was a very good rider, and thoughtful too. When he came home, the lady was at the hall door as he rode up.

"Well, my dear," she said, "how do you like him?"

"He is exactly what John said," he replied. "A more pleasant creature I never wish to mount. What shall we call him?"

"Do you like Ebony?" she said. "He is as black as ebony."

"No, not Ebony."

"How about Blackbird, like your uncle's old horse?"

"No, he is far handsomer than old Blackbird ever was."

"Yes," she said, "he is really quite a beauty, and he has such a sweet, good-tempered face and such fine intelligent eyes.

How about naming him Black Beauty?"

"Black Beauty - why, yes, I think that is a very good name. If you like, it shall be his name." And so it was.

John seemed very proud of me. He used to make my mane and tail almost as smooth as a lady's hair, and he talked to me a great deal. I grew very fond of him, he was so gentle and kind. He seemed to know just how a horse feels.

James Howard, the stable boy, was also gentle and pleasant, so I thought myself very well off.

A few days after this, I had to go out with Ginger in the carriage. I wondered how well we would get along, but she behaved very well.

She did her work honestly, and did her full share. I could not wish for a

better partner in double harness. When we came to a hill, instead of slacken-
ing her pace, she would throw her weight right into the collar and pull.

We both had the same sort of courage at our work, and John had to more
often hold us in than to urge us forward. He never had to use the whip with
either of us. Our paces were very much the same, and I found it very easy to
keep step with her when trotting, which made it pleasant. After we had been
out two or three times together we grew quite friendly and sociable, which
made me feel very much at home.

As for Merrylegs, my other stable mate, he and I became good friends.
He was such a cheerful, good-tempered little fellow that he was a favorite
with everyone, especially Jessie and Flora, who used to ride him about in the
orchard, and play games with him and their little dog Frisky.

Chapter V
LIBERTY AND GINGER

I was happy in my new place. I liked the people and the animals around me; everyone was good, and I had a light, airy stable and the best of food. What more could I want? There was something more, something much more important than anything else. It was Liberty! For three and a half years of my life I had all of the liberty I could possibly want. Now, week after week, month after month, and no doubt year after year, I must stand up in a stable night and day except when I am wanted, and then I must be just as steady and quiet as any old horse who has worked twenty years; straps here and straps there, a bit in my mouth, and blinkers over my eyes.

It's hard on a young horse full of strength and spirit who has been living in large fields and meadows, where he can fling up his head and toss his tail and gallop away at full speed, around and back again, with a snort to his companions; it's hard never to have liberty to do as you like. Sometimes, when I had less exercise than usual, I felt so full of life and spring that when John took me out to exercise I really could not keep quiet; it seemed as if I must jump, or dance, or prance, and many a good shake I know I must have given him, especially at first.

"Steady, my boy," he would say. "Wait a bit, and we'll have a good run. Soon we'll get the tickle out of your feet." Then as soon as we were out of the village, he would give me a few miles at a trot, and then bring me back as fresh as before, only clear of the fidgets, as he called them. Spirited horses, when not exercised enough, are often called skittish, when it is only play; and some grooms will punish them, but our John did not, he knew it was only high spirits. Still, he had his own ways of making me understand by the tone of his voice or the touch of the rein.

The carriage never went out on Sundays because the church was not far off. It was a great treat to us to be turned out into the home paddock or the old orchard. The grass was so cool and soft to our feet, the air so sweet, and the freedom to do as we liked was so pleasant; to gallop, to lie down and roll over on our backs, or to nibble the sweet grass. Also, it was a very good time for talking, as we stood together under the shade of the large chestnut tree.

One day when Ginger and I were out in the shade we had a long talk; she wanted to know all about my bringing up and breaking in, and I told her.

"Well," said she, "if I had your bringing up I might have had as good a temper as yours, but now I don't believe I ever shall."

"Why not?" I said.

"Because it has been so different for me," she replied. "I never had anyone, horse or man, that was kind to me. In the first place I was taken from my mother as soon as I was weaned and put with a lot of young colts. None of them cared for me, and I cared for none of them. There was no kind master like yours to look after me, and talk to me, and bring me nice things to eat. The man in charge of us never gave me a kind word in my life. I do not mean that he ill-used me, but he did not care for us one bit further than to see that we had food to eat and shelter in the winter.

We had fun running free in the meadows, galloping up and down, and chasing each other around the field. But when it came to breaking in, that was a bad time for me. Several men came to catch me, and when at last they closed in on me, one caught me by the forelock, another caught by the

22

nose and held it so tight I could hardly breathe. Then another took my underjaw in his hard hand and wrenched my mouth open; and so by force they got on the halter and bit into my mouth. Then one dragged me along by the halter, another flogging me from behind, it was all by force. They did not give me a chance to know what they wanted. I had a good deal of spirit and gave them, I dare say, plenty of trouble; but it was dreadful to be shut up in a stall day after day instead of being free, and I fretted and wanted to get loose. It's bad enough when you have a kind master and plenty of coaxing, but there was nothing of that sort for me.

Chapter VI
PLAIN SPEAKING

The longer I lived at Birtwick Hall, the more proud and happy I felt. Our master and mistress were respected and beloved by all who knew them. They were kind to everybody and everything; not only men and women, but horses, donkeys, dogs, cats, cattle and birds. There was no oppressed or ill-used creature that had not a friend in them. If any of the local children were known to treat any creature cruelly, they soon heard about it from the Hall.

I remember one morning when our master was riding me towards home, when we saw a powerful man driving ahead of us in a light pony cart, driving a beautiful little bay pony, who had slender legs and a highbred sensitive head and face. Just as he came close to our gate, the little pony turned towards it. The man, without word or warning, wrenched the pony's head back with such force and suddenness that he nearly threw it on it's haunches.

Recovering itself, it was continuing on when he began to lash at it furiously. The pony plunged forward, but the strong, heavy hand held the pretty creature back with force almost enough to break it's jaw, while the whip still cut into him. It was a dreadful sight to see, for I knew what fearful pain it gave that delicate little mouth.

The master signalled me, and we caught up with them in a few seconds.

"Sawyer," he cried in a stern voice, "is that pony made of flesh and blood?"

"Flesh and blood and temper," he said. "He's too fond of his own will, and that doesn't suit me," he said angrily.

"And do you think," said the master sternly, "that treatment like this will make him fond of your will?"

"He had no business to make that turn; his road was straight on," said the man roughly.

"You have often driven that pony up to my place," said my master. "It only shows the creature has memory and intelligence. How did he know that you were not going there again? But that has little to do with it. I must say, Mr. Sawyer, that more unmanly, brutal treatment of a little pony it was never my painful lot to witness; and by giving way to such passion you injure your horse. Remember, we shall all have to be judged according to our works, whether they be towards man or towards beast."

Master rode me home slowly, and I could sense how the incident grieved him.

Chapter VII
A STORMY DAY

One day late in autumn, my master took a long journey on business. I was hitched to the dogcart, and John went with us. There had been a great deal of rain, and now the wind was high and blew the leaves across the road in a shower. We were fine until we came to the toll bar at the low wooden bridge. Here the river banks were high, and the bridge, instead of arching, stretched across level, so that in the middle, if the river was full, the water would be nearly up to the woodwork and planks.

The man at the gate said the river was rising fast and he feared it would be a bad night. Many of the meadows were under water, and in one low part of the road, the water was halfway up to my knees.

When we got to the town, I had a good meal and a rest. The master's business took a long time and we didn't start for home till rather late in the afternoon. The wind was much higher by then, and I heard the master say to John that he had never been out in such a storm. As we went along the edge of the forest, the great branches were swaying about like little twigs, and the strong wind rushing through the leaves sounded eerie.

"I'll be glad to be out of these woods," said my master.

"Yes, sir," said John, "Just one of those branches could do a lot of harm."

The words were scarcely out of his mouth, when there was a groan, and a crack, and a splitting sound; and tearing, and crashing down among the other trees came an oak. It fell across the road right in front of us. I won't say that I wasn't frightened, for I was terrified. I stopped still, trembling; but did not turn or run away. John jumped out and was at my head in a moment .

"Almost an accident," said my master. "What now?"

"Well, sir, we can't drive over that tree nor get around it; there's nothing we can do but go back to the crossroad, and it will be a good six miles before we get around to the wooden bridge again. It will make us late."

So back we went to the crossroad; but by the time we got to the bridge it was almost dark. We could see that the water was over the middle of it. As that happened sometimes when the floods were out, master did not stop. We were going along at a good pace, but the moment my feet touched the first part of the bridge I felt sure there was something wrong. I dared not go forward, and I made a dead stop. "Go on, Beauty," said my master, but I dared not stir. He gave me a touch of the whip. I moved, but I dared not go forward.

"There's something wrong, sir," said John, and he sprang out of the dogcart, looked all about, and tried to lead me forward.

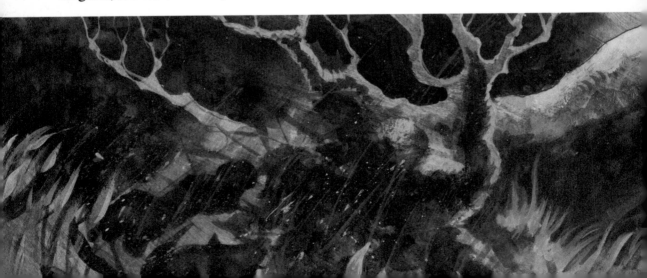

"Come on, Beauty, what's the matter?" I could not tell him, but I sensed that the bridge was not safe.

Just then the man at the tollgate ran out waving a lantern like a mad man.

"Hey, hey, hello, stop!" he cried.

"What's the matter?" shouted my master.

"The bridge is broken in the middle, and part of it is carried away. If you come on you'll be into the river."

"Thank God!" said my master. "You Beauty!" said John, and took the bridle and gently turned me around. The sun had set, and the wind seemed to have slowed down after that furious blast which tore up the tree. It grew darker and darker, and very quiet. I trotted along, the wheels hardly making a sound on the soft road. For a good while neither master nor John spoke, and then master began in a serious voice to say that if I had gone on as he had wanted me to; horse, dog cart, master and man would have fallen into the river; and as the current was flowing very strongly, and there was no light and no help at hand, it was likely we would all have drowned. Master said God

had given men reason, by which they could find things out by themselves, but he had given animals instinct which did not depend on reason, and was more prompt and perfect in its way, and by which it had often saved lives. John had many stories to tell of dogs and horses, and the wonderful things they had done. He thought people did not value their animals half enough, nor make friends of them as they should.

At last we came to the park gates, and found the gardener looking for us. He said the mistress had been in a dreadful state, fearing some accident had happened.

As we came up the mistress ran out, saying, "Are you really safe, my dear? Have you had an accident?"

"No, my dear, but if your Black Beauty had not been wiser than we were, we should all have been carried down the river at the wooden bridge." I heard no more, as they went into the house, and John took me to the stable. Oh! what a good supper he gave me that night, and such a thick bed of straw, and I was glad for it because I was very tired.

Chapter VIII
THE FIRE

One day it was decided by my master and mistress to pay a visit to some friends in a nearby town, and James was to drive them. The first day we traveled over thirty miles; there were some long, heavy hills, but James drove so carefully and thoughtfully that we were not at all harassed. He never forgot to put on the drag as we went downhill, nor to take it off at the right place. He kept our feet on the smoothest part of the road, and if the uphill was very long, he set the carriage wheels a little across the road, so as not to run back, and thereby gave us a breathing. All these things help a horse very much, particularly if he gets kind words in the bargain.

Just as the sun was going down we reached the town where we were to spend the night. We stopped at the principal hotel in the market place. We drove under an archway into a long yard, with stables and coach houses at the far end. Two grooms came to meet us. One was a pleasant, active little man, with a crooked leg and a yellow striped waistcoat. He unbuckled my harness quickly, and with a pat and a good word led me to a long stable, with six or eight stalls in it and two or three horses.

The other man brought Ginger. James stood by while we were rubbed down and cleaned.

Later on in the evening a traveler's horse was brought in by the second groom, and while he was cleaning him a young man with a pipe in his mouth wandered into the stable to gossip.

"I say, Towler," said the groom, "run up the ladder to the loft and put some hay down into this horse's rack, will you? Only lay down your pipe."

"All right," said Towler, and he went up through the trap door. I heard him step across the floor overhead and put down the hay. James came in to look at us the last thing, and then the door was locked.

I cannot say how long I had slept, nor what time in the night it was, but I woke up very uncomfortable, though I hardly knew why. I got up and the air seemed thick and choking. I heard Ginger coughing, and one of the other horses moved about restlessly. It was quite dark, and I could see nothing, but the stable was full of smoke and I could hardly breathe.

I thought the smoke was coming from the direction of the trap door which had been left open. I listened and heard a soft rushing sort of noise, and a low crackling and snapping. I did not know what it was, but there was something in the sound so frightening I began to tremble. The other horses were now all awake; some were pulling at their halters, others were stamping.

At last the groom who had put up the other horses burst into the stable with a lantern, and began to untie us. He tried to lead one out; but he was in such a hurry and seemed so frightened himself that the horse would not go with him; he tried the second and third, but they would not stir.

He came to me next and tried to drag me out of the stall by force, but it was no use. He tried us all by turns and then left the stable.

No doubt we were foolish, but danger seemed to be all around, and there was nobody we knew to trust. Everything was strange and uncertain. Fresh air that had come in through the open door made it easier to breathe, but the rushing sound overhead grew louder, and as I looked upward through the bars of my empty rack I saw a red light flickering on the wall. I heard a cry of "Fire" outside, and suddenly the old groom appeared. He managed to get one horse out and went to another. The flames were playing around the trap door, and the roaring overhead was awful.

The next thing I heard was James' voice, quiet and cheery, as always.

"Come, my beauties, it is time for us to be off, so wake up and come along." I stood nearest the door, so he came to me first, patting me as he came in. "Come, Beauty, on with your bridle, my boy, we'll soon be out of this smother." It was on in no time, then he took the scarf off his neck, and tied it lightly over my eyes, and patting and coaxing he led me out of the stable. Safe in the yard, he slipped the scarf off my eyes and shouted, "Here, somebody, take this horse, I have to go back for another."

A tall, broad man stepped forward and took me, and James darted back into the stable. I set up a shrill whinny as I saw him go. Ginger told me afterwards that my whinny was the best thing I could have done for her, for had she not heard me outside she wouldn't have had the courage to come out.

There was much confusion in the yard, the horses being taken out of other stables, and the carriages and carts being pulled out of their sheds, lest the flames should spread further. On the other side of the yard, windows were thrown up, and people were shouting all sorts of things; but I kept my eyes fixed on the stable door, where the smoke poured out thicker than ever, and I could see flashes of red light. Then I heard above all the stir and din, a loud, clear voice, which I knew was master's:

"James Howard! James Howard! Are you there?" There was no answer, but I heard a crash of something falling in the stable, and the next moment

I gave a loud, joyful neigh, for I saw James coming through the smoke leading Ginger with him; she was coughing violently, and he was not able to speak.

"My brave lad!" said my master, laying his hand on James' shoulder. "Are you hurt?"

James shook his head, for he could not yet speak.

"Yes," said the big man who held me, "he is a brave lad."

Suddenly from the marketplace came the sound of galloping feet and loud rumbling wheels.

"It's the fire engine, the fire engine!" shouted two or three voices, "Stand back, make way!" And clattering and thundering over the stones, two horses dashed into the yard with the heavy engine behind them. The fireman leaped to the ground; there was no need to ask where the fire was - it was torching up in a great blaze from the roof.

As they began to battle the roaring flames, James and my master led Ginger and me out of the courtyard and across the marketplace to another hotel where my mistress was waiting, overjoyed to see that we were all safe.

Chapter IX
GOING FOR THE DOCTOR

One night, several months later, I had eaten my hay and was lying down in my straw fast asleep, when I was suddenly roused by the stable bell ringing loudly. I heard the door of John's house open, and his feet running up to the Hall. He was back again in no time. He unlocked the stable door and came in, calling out: "Wake up, Beauty, we're going for a gallop," and almost before I could think he had the saddle on my back and the bridle on my head. He grabbed a coat, and then ran with me on a quick trot up to the Hall door. The Squire stood there with a lamp in his hand.

"Now, John," he said, "ride for your life, that is, for your mistress's life. There is not a moment to lose; give this note to Doctor White; give your horse a rest at the inn, and be back as soon as you can."

John said, "Yes, sir," and was on my back. The gardener who lived at the lodge had heard the bell ring, and was ready with the gate open, and away we went through the Park and through the village, and down the hill till we came to the toll-gate. John called out loudly while banging on the door. A man soon appeared and flung open the gate.

"Please keep the gate open for the doctor," said John. "Here's the money," and we were off again at top speed.

Before us lay a long stretch of level road along the riverside. John said to me, "Now, Beauty, do your best," and so I did; I needed no whip or spur, and for two miles I galloped as fast as I could. I don't believe that my old grandfather who won the race at Newmarket could have gone faster. When we came to the bridge, John pulled me up a little and patted my neck. "Well done, Beauty! good fellow," he said. He would have let me go slower, but my spirit was up, and I was off again as fast as before.

The air was frosty, the moon was bright, and it was very pleasant. We came through a village, then through a dark wood, then uphill, then downhill, till after an eight mile run we came to the town, through the streets and into the marketplace. It was all quite still except for the clatter of my feet on the stones. Everybody was asleep. The church clock struck three as we drew up to Doctor White's door. John rang the bell twice, and then pounded on the door. A window was thrown up, and Doctor White, in his nightcap, put his head out and said, "Who's there? What's the matter?"

"It's John Manley, sir. Mrs. Gordon is very ill; master wants you to come at once. He thinks she will die if you cannot get there. Here is a note."

"Wait," he said, "I'm coming."

He shut the window, and soon was at the door.

"There's a problem," Dr. White said. "My horse has been out all day and is quite worn out. My son has just been sent for, and has taken the other horse. May I take yours?"

"He has come at a gallop nearly the whole way, sir, and I was to give him a rest here. I think, however, my master would not be against it if you think it's alright, sir."

"All right," he said, "I'll soon be ready."

John stood by me and stroked my neck; I was very hot. The doctor came out with his riding whip.

"You need not take that, sir," said John, "Black Beauty will go till he

drops. Take care of him, sir, if you can; I should not want any harm to come to him."

"No! no! John," said the doctor, "I hope not," and in a minute we had left John far behind.

I will not tell about our way back; the doctor was a heavier man than John, and not so good a rider; however, I did my very best. The man at the toll-gate had it open. When we came to the hill, the doctor drew me up. "Now, my good fellow," he said, "take some breath." I was glad he did, for I was nearly spent, but the breathing spell helped me, and soon we were in the Park. Joe was at the gate, and my master was at the Hall door. He spoke not a word. The doctor went into the house with him, and Joe led me to the stable.

I was glad to get home, my legs shook under me, and I could only stand and pant. I had not a dry hair on my body, the water ran down my legs, and I steamed all over.

Poor Joe! He was young, and as yet knew very little about horses. His father, who would have helped him, had been sent to the next village. I am sure he did the very best he knew. He rubbed my legs and my chest, but he did not put my warm cloth on me. He thought I was so hot I wouldn't like it. Then he gave me a pailful of water to drink; it was cold and very good, and I drank it all. Then he gave me some hay and some corn, and thinking he had done right, he went away. Soon I began to shake and tremble, and turned deadly cold, my legs ached, and I felt sore all over. Oh! how I wished for my warm thick cloth as I stood and trembled. I wished for John, but he had eight miles to walk, so I lay down in my straw and tried to go to sleep.

After a long while I heard John at the door; I gave a low moan, for I was in great pain. He was at my side in a moment, stooping down by me. I could not tell him how I felt, but he seemed to know. He appeared upset. I heard him say to himself over and over again, "Stupid boy! Stupid boy! No cloth put on, and I dare say the water was cold too." He covered me up with two or three warm cloths, and then ran to the house for some hot water. He made me some warm gruel, which I drank, and then I went to sleep.

I was now very ill. A strong inflammation had attacked my lungs, and I could not draw my breath without pain. John nursed me night and day. He would get up a couple times in the night to come to me. "My poor Beauty," he said one day, "good old horse, you saved your mistress's life." I was very glad to hear that. The doctor had said if we had been a little longer it would have been too late. John told my master he had never seen a horse go so fast in his life, and it seemed as if the horse knew what was the matter. I knew as much as this, that John and I must go at top speed, and that it was for the sake of the mistress.

I do not know how long I was ill. Mr. Bond, the horse doctor, came every day. Ginger and Merrylegs had been moved into another stable so that I might be quiet, for the fever made my hearing very keen. Any little noise seemed quite loud, and I could tell everyone's footsteps from the house.

One night John had to give me medication. Thomas Green came in to help him. After I had taken it and John had made me as comfortable as he could, he said he should stay half an hour to see how the medicine settled.

Thomas said he would stay with him, so they went and sat down on a bench that had been brought into Merryleg's stall, and put down the lantern at their feet that I might not be disturbed by the light.

For awhile both men sat silent, and then Tom Green said in a low voice:

"I wish, John, you'd say a kind word to Joe. The boy is quite broken-hearted. He can't eat his meals, and he can't smile. He says he knows it was all his fault, though he is sure he did the best he knew, and he says, if Beauty dies, no one will ever speak to him again. It goes to my heart to hear him; I think you might give him just a word. He is not a bad boy."

After a short pause, John said slowly, "You must not be too hard on me, Tom. I know he meant no harm, I never said he did. I know he is not a bad boy, but you see I am sore myself. That horse is the pride of my heart, to say nothing of his being such a favorite with the master and mistress; and to think that his life may be flung away in this manner is more than I can bear; but if you think I am hard on the boy I will try to give him a good word tomorrow - that is, I mean, if Beauty is better."

Chapter X
JOE GREEN

Joe Green worked out very well. He learned quickly, and was so atten-
tive and careful that John began to trust him for many things; but, as I have
said, he was young, and it was rare that he was allowed to exercise Ginger or
me. But it so happened one morning that John was out in the luggage cart,
and the master wanted a note taken immediately to a gentleman's house, about
three miles distant, and sent his orders for Joe to saddle me and take it, adding
the caution that he was to ride carefully.

All went well, the note was delivered, and we were quietly returning
when we came to the brickfield. Here we saw a cart heavily laden with
bricks. The wheels had stuck fast in the stiff mud of some deep ruts, and the
driver was shouting and flogging the two horses unmercifully. Joe pulled up.
It was a sad sight . There were the two horses straining and struggling with all
their might to drag the cart, but they could not move it. The sweat streamed
from their legs and flanks, their sides heaved, and every muscle strained,
while the man swore fiercely and lashed most brutally.

"Hold hard," said Joe, "don't go on flogging the horses like that; the wheels are so stuck that they can't move the cart." The man took no heed, but went on lashing.

"Stop!" said Joe. "I'll help lighten the cart; they can't move it now."

"Mind your own business, you impudent young rascal," said the man, in a towering passion, as he laid on the whip again.

Joe turned my head, and the next moment we were going at a gallop toward the house of the master brickmaker. I cannot say if John would have approved of our pace, but Joe and I were both of one mind, and so angry that we could not have gone slower.

The house stood close by the roadside. Joe knocked at the door and shouted, "Hello! Is Mr. Clay at home?" The door was opened, and Mr. Clay himself came out.

"Hello, young man! You seem in a hurry; any orders from the Squire this morning?"

"No, Mr. Clay, but there's a fellow in your brickyard flogging two horses to death. I told him to stop but he wouldn't. I said I'd help him to lighten the cart, but he wouldn't. So I have come to tell you; please go, sir." Joe's voice shook with concern.

"Thank you, lad," said the man, "Will you give evidence of what you have seen if I should bring this fellow up before a magistrate?"

"I will," said Joe, as the man left. We then started home at a smart trot.

"Why, what's the matter, Joe?" said John, as the boy flung himself from the saddle.

"I'm so angry, I can tell you," said the boy, and then in hurried, excited words he told all that had happened. Joe was usually such a quiet, gentle fellow that it was wonderful to see him so roused.

"Right, Joe! You did right, my boy, whether the fellow gets a summons or not. Many folks would have ridden by and said it was not their business to interfere. I say with cruelty and oppression it's everybody's business to interfere. You did right, my boy."

Chapter XI
THE PARTING

I had now lived in this happy place three years, but sad changes were about to come over us. We heard from time to time that our mistress was ill. The doctor was often at our house, and the master looked grave and anxious. Then we heard that she must leave her home at once and go to a warm country for two or three years. The news fell upon the household like the tolling of a death bell. The master immediately began making arrangements for selling his establishment and leaving England. We used to hear it talked about in our stable; indeed, nothing else was talked about.

John went about his work silent and sad, and Joe scarcely whistled. There was a great deal of coming and going; Ginger and I had lots of work.

The first of the party who went were Jessie and Flora with their governess. They came to bid us good-bye. They hugged us all and threw their arms around Merryleg's neck, and cried into his mane. Then we heard what had been arranged for us. Master had sold Ginger and me to his old friend, the Earl of W, for he thought we should have a good place there. Merrylegs he had given to the Minister, who was wanting a pony for his wife, but it was on the condition that he should never be sold.

Chapter XII
EARLSHALL PARK

The next morning after breakfast, Joe put Merrylegs into the mistress' low cart to deliver him to the church. He came first and said good-bye to us, and Merrylegs neighed to us from the yard. Then John put the saddle on Ginger and the leading rein on me, and rode us across the country about fifteen miles to Earlshall Park, where the Earl of W lived.

We were taken to a light, airy stable, and placed in boxes adjoining each other, where we were rubbed down and fed. In about half an hour John and Mr. York, who was to be our new coachman, came in to see us.

"Now, Mr. Manly," he said, after carefully looking at us both, "I can see no fault in these horses, but we all know that horses have their peculiarities as well as people, and that sometimes they need different treatment. I should like to know if there is anything particular in either of these that you would like to mention."

"Well," said John, "I don't believe there is a better pair of horses in the country, and I am sad to part with them, but they are not alike.

The black one has the most perfect temper I've ever known. I expect he has never known a hard word or felt a blow since he was foaled, for all his pleasure seems to be to do what you wish. The chestnut I fancy must have had bad treatment. We heard as much from the dealer. She came to us snappish and suspicious, but when she found what sort of place ours was, she slowly calmed down. For three years I have never seen the smallest sign of temper, and if she is well treated you could not find a better, more willing animal. She naturally has a more irritable constitution than the black horse. Flies tease her more. Anything wrong in the harness frets her more, and if she were ill-used or unfairly treated she would likely give tit for tat. You know that many high-mettled horses will do so."

"Of course," said York, "I quite understand, but you know it's not easy in stables like these to have all the grooms just what they should be. I do my best, and there I must leave it. I'll remember what you have said about the mare."

"I am sorry to leave them, very sorry," said John.

He came around to each of us to pat and speak to us for the last time. His voice sounded very sad.

I held my face close to him. That was all I could do to say good-bye. And then he was gone.

Chapter XIII
REUBEN SMITH

I must now say a little about Reuben Smith, who was left in charge of the stables when our coachman, York, went to London. No one more thoroughly understood his business than Smith did, and when he was all right, there could not be a more faithful or valuable man.

He was gentle and very clever in his management of horses, and could doctor them almost as well as a veterinarian, for he had lived two years with a veterinary surgeon. He was a first-rate driver too. He could handle a four-in-hand or a tandem as easily as a pair. He was a handsome man, a good scholar, and had very pleasant manners. I believe everybody liked him, certainly the horses did.

The only wonder was that he was in a lower position, and not in the place of a head coachman, like York. But he had one great fault, and that was the love of drink.

One night, when Reuben had to drive a party home from a dance, he was drunk and could not hold the reins. A gentleman of the party had to mount the box and drive the ladies home, and Reuben was at once dismissed and his wife and little children had to leave the pretty cottage by the Park gate. This had happened a good while ago; and shortly before Ginger and I came, Smith had been taken back again. York had interceded for him with the Earl, who is very kind-hearted, and Reuben had promised faithfully that he would never taste another drop as long as he lived. He had kept his promise so well that York thought he might be safely trusted to fill his place while he was away.

It was now early April, and the family was expected home some time in May. The light carriage was to be freshly painted in town, and as the Colonel was obliged to return to his regiment, it was arranged that Smith should drive him to town in it, and ride me back. For this purpose, he took the saddle with him. At the station the Colonel put some money into Smith's hand and bid him good-bye, saying, "Take care of your young mistress, Reuben, and don't let Black Beauty be hacked about by any random young person who wants to ride him. Keep him for the lady."

We left the carriage at the maker's to be painted, and Smith rode me to the White Lion and ordered the groom to feed me well and have me ready for him at four o'clock. A nail in one of my front shoes had started to loosen. The groom didn't notice it till just about four o'clock. Smith did not come into the yard till five, and then he said he would not leave till six, as he had met some old friends. The man then told him of the nail, and asked if he should have the shoe fixed.

"No," said Smith, "that will be all right till we get home."

He spoke in a very loud, offhand way, and it was very unlike him not to see about the shoe, as he was generally very particular about loose nails in our shoes. He did not come at six, nor seven, nor eight, and it was nearly nine o'clock before he called for me, and then it was in a loud, rough voice. He seemed in a very bad temper, and abused the groom, though for what reason, I could not tell.

The landlord stood at the door and said, "Take care, Mr. Smith!" But he answered angrily, and almost before he was out of the town, he began to gallop; frequently giving me a sharp cut with his whip, though I was going at full speed. The moon had not yet risen, and it was very dark. The roads were

stony, having been recently mended. Going over them at this pace, my shoe became looser, and when we were near the turnpike gate, it came off. If Smith had been in his right senses, he would have noticed something wrong in my pace; but he was too drunk to notice anything.

Beyond the turnpike there was a long stretch of road, upon which fresh stones had just been laid, large sharp stones, over which no horse could be driven quickly without risk of danger. Over this road, with one shoe gone, I was forced to gallop at my utmost speed; my rider meanwhile cutting into me with his whip, and with wild curses urging me to go still faster. Of course my shoeless foot suffered dreadfully; the hoof was broken and split down to the very quick, and the inside was terribly cut by the sharpness of the stones.

No horse could keep his footing under such circumstances, the pain was too great. I stumbled, and fell with violence on both my knees. Smith was flung off by my fall, and owing to the speed I was going, must have fallen with great force. I scrambled back to my feet and limped to the side of the road, where it was free from stones.

The moon had just risen above the hedge, and by it's light I could see Smith lying a few yards beyond me. He tried to rise but fell back with a heavy groan. There was one more faint gasp from Smith, but after that I could see no motion, though he lay in full moonlight.

Chapter XIV
HOW IT ENDED

It must have been nearly midnight when I heard the faint sound of horse's feet. Sometimes the sound died away, then it grew louder again and nearer. The road to Earlshall led through plantations that belonged to the Earl. The sound came from that direction, and I hoped it might be someone coming in search for us. As the sound came nearer and nearer, I was almost sure I could distinguish Ginger's step; a little nearer still, and I could tell she was pulling the dogcart. I neighed loudly, and was overjoyed to hear an answering neigh from Ginger, and men's voices. They came slowly over the stones, and stopped at the dark figure that lay upon the ground.

One of the men jumped out, and stooped down over it. "It's Reuben!" he said, "and he does not stir."

The other man followed and bent over him. "He's dead," he said; "no pulse at all."

They raised him up, but he was lifeless, and his hair was soaked with blood. They laid him down again, and came and looked at me. They soon saw my cut knees.

"Why, the horse has been down and thrown him! Who would have

thought the black horse would have done that? Nobody thought he could fall.
Reuben must have been lying here for hours! Odd, too, that the horse has not
moved from the place."

Robert tried to lead me forward. I made a step, but almost fell again.

"Oh, Oh! He's bad in his foot as well as his knees. Look here - his hoof
is cut all to pieces. He might well fall down, poor fellow! I tell you what,
Ned, I'm afraid it hasn't been all right with Reuben. Just think of him riding a
horse over these stones without a shoe! Why, if he had been in his right
senses he would just as soon have tried to ride him over the moon. I'm afraid
it has been the old thing over again. Poor Susan! She looked awfully pale
when she came to my house to ask if he had not come home. She made
believe she was not a bit anxious, and talked of a lot of things that might have
kept him. But for all that, she begged me to go and meet him. Now we must
get him home - and the horse as well."

Then followed a conversation between them, till it was agreed that
Robert, as the groom, should lead me, and that Ned must take the body.

Ned started off very slowly with his sad load, and Robert came and
looked at my foot again. Then he took his handkerchief and bound it closely
around it, and then he led me home. I shall never forget that night walk; it
was more than three miles. Robert led me on very slowly, and I limped and
hobbled on as well as I could with great pain. I am sure he was sorry for me,
for he often patted and encouraged me, talking to me in a pleasant voice.

At last I reached my box, and had some corn. And after Robert had
wrapped up my knees in wet cloths, he tied up my foot in bran poultice to
draw out the heat and cleanse it before the horse doctor saw it in the morning
Then I managed to get myself down on the straw in spite of the pain.

The next day, the vetenarian examined my injuries. He said he hoped the
joint was not injured; and if so, I should not be spoiled for work, but I should
never lose the blemish. I believe they did the best to make a good cure, but it
was a long and painful one.

Because Smith's death had been so sudden, and there had been no witness to it, an inquest was held. The landlord and the groom at the White Lion, and several others gave evidence that he was intoxicated when he left the inn. The keeper of the toll-gate said he rode at a hard gallop through the gate. My shoe was picked up among the stones. The cause of death was quite evident, and I was absolved of all blame.

Chapter XV
RUINED, AND GOING DOWNHILL

As soon as my knees were sufficiently healed, I was turned into a small meadow for a month or two. No other creature was there, and though I enjoyed the liberty and the sweet grass, I had been used to society so long that I felt very lonely. Ginger and I had become fast friends, and now I missed her company very much.

I often neighed when I heard horses' hoofs passing in the road, but I seldom got an answer. Then one morning the gate was opened, and I was overjoyed to see dear old Ginger coming through.

The man slipped off her halter and left her there. With a joyful whinny I trotted up to her. We were both delighted to meet, but I soon found that it was not for our pleasure that she was brought to be with me. The sad truth was that she had been ruined by hard riding, and was now being put out to pasture to see if a good rest would do any good.

It seems that the Earl's son, Lord George, was a very hard rider, and quite careless of his horses. He loved to hunt whenever he got the chance. Soon after I left the stable there was a steeplechase, and he determined to ride.

Though the groom had told him Ginger was a little strained, and not at all ready for such a race, he refused to believe it, and on the day of the race urged Ginger to go her fastest.

With her great spirit, Ginger strained herself to the utmost. She came in with the first three horses, but her wind was touched, and because Lord George was much too heavy for her, her back was strained. "And so," she said, "here we are - ruined in the prime of our youth and strength - you by a drunk and I by a fool. It's very sad."

We both felt in ourselves that we were not what we had been. However, that did not spoil the pleasure we had in each other's company. We did not gallop about as we once did, but we used to feed, and lie down together, and stand for hours under one of the shady lime trees with our heads close to each other; and so we passed our time till the family returned.

One day we saw the Earl come into the meadow, York was with him. Seeing who it was, we stood still, and let them come up to us. They examined us carefully. The Earl seemed much annoyed.

"There is three hundred pounds flung away for no earthly use," said he, "but what is worse is that these horses of my old friend, who thought they would find a good home with me, are ruined. The mare shall have a twelve-month's run, and we shall see what that will do for her; but the black one must be sold. It's a great pity, but I could not have knees like these in my stables."

"No, my lord, of course not," said York, "but he might get a place where appearance is not of much consequence, and still be well treated. I know a man who is the master of some livery stables, who often wants a good horse at a low figure. I know he looks after his horses well. The inquest cleared the horse's character, and your recommendation, or mine, would be sufficient warrant for him."

"Please write to him, York. I am much more particular about the place than the money he would bring."

After this they left us.

"They'll take you away," said Ginger, "and I shall lose my best friend."

About a week after this, Robert came into the field with a halter, which he slipped over my head, and led me away.

Ginger and I neighed to each other as I was led off, and she trotted anxiously along the hedge, watching me go.

Through the recommendation of York I was bought by the master of the livery stables. I had to go by train, which was new to me, and required a good deal of courage the first time.

When I reached the end of my journey I found myself in a comfortable stable. These stables were not as airy and pleasant as those I had before. They were laid on a slope instead of being level, and as my head was kept tied to the trough, I was obliged always to stand on the slope, which was very fatiguing. Horses can do more work if they can stand level and turn about. He kept a good many horses and carriages of different kinds for hire. Sometimes his own men drove them; at other times, the horse and cart were rented to gentlemen or ladies who drove themselves.

Some of these riders, instead of starting at an easy pace as a gentle person would do, set off at full speed from the stable yard; and when they wanted to stop, they would first whip us, and then pull up so suddenly that we were nearly thrown on our haunches, and our mouths slashed with the bit. They called that "pulling up with a dash;" and when they turned a corner, they did it as sharply as if there were no right side or wrong side of the road.

I well remember one spring evening Robby and I had been out for the day. (Robby was the horse that usually went with me when a pair was ordered.) We had our own driver, and were coming home at a good smart pace about twilight. Our road turned sharply to the left, but as we were close to the hedge on our side, and there was plenty of room to pass, our driver did not pull us in. As we neared the corner I heard a horse and two wheels coming rapidly down the hill towards us. The hedge was high and I could see nothing, but the next moment we were upon each other. Happily for me, I was on the side next to the hedge.

Robby was on the other side, and had nothing to protect him. The man who was driving was going straight for the corner, and when he came in sight of us he had no time to pull over to his side. The whole blow came upon Robby. The cart shaft ran right into his chest, making him stagger back with a loud cry. The other horse was thrown down, and one shaft was broken.

There was poor Robby with his flesh torn and bleeding. They said if it had been a little more to one side, it would have killed him.

It was a long time before the wound healed, and then he was sold for coal carting. What that is, up and down those steep hills, only horses know.

Of course we sometimes had good driving. I remember one morning I was put into the light cart, and taken to a house in Pulham Street. A gentleman came out and came round to my head; he looked at the bit and bridle, and shifted the collar with his hand to see if it fitted comfortably.

Then he took the reins, and got up. I can remember now how quietly he turned me around, and then with a light feel of the rein, we were off.

I arched my neck and set off at my best pace. I found I had someone behind me who knew how a good horse ought to be driven. It seemed like old times again, and made me feel quite happy.

This gentleman took a great liking to me, and he prevailed upon my master to sell me to a friend of his, who wanted a safe, pleasant horse for riding. And so it came to pass that in summer I was sold to Mr. Barry.

Chapter XVI
A THIEF

My new master was an unmarried man. He lived in Kent, and was much engaged in business. His doctor had advised him to take more exercise, and for this purpose he bought me. He rented a stable a short distance from his home, and engaged a man named Filcher as groom.

My master knew very little about horses, but he treated me well, and I should have had a good and easy place but for circumstances of which he was ignorant. He ordered the best hay with plenty of oats, crushed beans, and bran with rye grass. The master gave the order, so there should have been plenty of good food, and I should have been well off.

For a few days all went well. I found that my groom understood his business. He kept the stable clean and airy, he groomed me thoroughly, and he was always gentle. He had been a groom in one of the great hotels in town, but he had given that up to cultivate fruits and vegetables for the market, and his wife bred and fattened poultry and rabbits for sale.

After a while it seemed to me that my oats came very short; I had the beans, but bran was mixed with them instead of oats, of which there were very

few; certainly not more than a quarter of what there should have been. In two or three weeks this began to tell upon my strength and spirits. The grass food, though very good, was not enough to keep up my condition without corn.

However, I could not complain, or make known my needs. So it went on for about two months, and I wondered why my master did not notice that something was the matter.

Then one afternoon we rode out into the country to see a friend of his, a farmer who lived on the road to Wells. This gentleman had a very good eye for horses, and after casting an eye over me:

"It seems to me, Barry, that your horse does not look so well as he did when you first had him. Has he been well?"

"Yes, I believe so," said my master, "but he is not nearly as lively as he was. My groom tells me that horses are always dull and weak in the autumn, and that I must expect it."

"Autumn! fiddlesticks! " said the farmer. "Why, this is only August, and with your light work and good food he shouldn't go down like this, even if it were autumn. How do you feed him?"

My master told him. His friend shook his head, and began to feel me.

"I can't say who eats the corn, my dear fellow, but I am much mistaken if your horse gets it. Have you ridden very fast?"

"No! very gently."

"Then just put your hand here," said he, passing his hand over my neck and shoulder. "He is as warm and damp as a horse just come up from grass. I advise you to look into your stable a little more. I hate to be suspicious, and thank heaven I have no cause to be, for I can trust my men present or absent, but there are mean scoundrels, wicked enough to rob a dumb beast of his food. You must look into it." And turning to his man who had come to take me, "Give this horse a right good feed of bruised oats, and don't stint him."

If I could have spoken I could have told my master where his corn went. My groom used to come every morning about six o'clock, and with him a little boy, who always had a covered basket with him. He'd go with his father into the harness room where the corn was kept, and I could see them, when the door was ajar, fill a little bag with corn out of the bin, and then he'd leave.

Five or six mornings after this, just as the boy had left the stable, the door was pushed open and a policeman walked in, holding the child tight by the arm; another policeman followed, and locked the door on the inside, saying, "Show me the place where your father keeps his rabbits' food."

The boy looked very frightened and began to cry; but there was no escape, and he led the way to the corn-bin. Here the policeman found another empty bag like that which was found full of corn in the boy's basket.

Filcher was cleaning my feet at the time, but they soon saw him, and though he blustered a great deal, they walked him off to the "lock-up," and his boy with him. I heard afterwards that the boy was not held to be guilty, but the man was sentenced to prison for two months.

Chapter XVII
A HUMBUG

My master was not immediately able to find a replacement, but in a few days my new groom came. He was a tall, good looking fellow; but if ever there was a humbug in the shape of a groom, Alfred Smirk was the man. He was very civil to me, and never ill-used me; in fact, he did a great deal of stroking and patting, when his master was there to see it. He always brushed my mane and tail with water, and my hoofs with oil before he brought me to the door, to make me look smart. But as to cleaning my feet, or looking to my shoes, or grooming me thoroughly, he thought no more of that than if I had been a cow. He left my bit rusty, and my saddle damp.

Alfred Smirk considered himself very handsome; he spent a great deal of time fixing his hair, moustache, and necktie before a little mirror in the harness room. When his master was speaking to him, it was always, "Yes, sir; yes, sir," touching his hat at every word. Everyone thought he was a very nice man, and that Mr. Barry was very fortunate to find him. Acually, he was the laziest, most conceited fellow imaginable.

Of course it was a great thing not to be ill-used, but then a horse needs more than that. I had a loose box, and might have been very comfortable if he had not been too lazy to clean it out. He never took all the straw away, and the smell from what lay underneath was very bad. The strong vapors that rose up made my eyes inflame, and I did not feel the same appetite for my food.

One day his master came in and said, "Alfred, the stable smells rather strong. Why don't you give that stall a good scrub, and throw down plenty of water?"

"Well, sir," he said, touching his cap, "I'll do so if you please , sir, but it is rather dangerous, sir, throwing down water in a horse's box; they are very apt to take cold, sir. I should not like to do him an injury, but I'll do it if you please, sir."

"Well," said the master, "I should not like him to take cold, but I don't like the smell of this stable. Do you think the drains are all right?"

"Well, sir, now that you mention it, I think the drain does sometimes send back a smell. There may be something wrong, sir."

"Then send for the bricklayer and have it seen to," said the master.

"Yes, sir, I will."

The bricklayer came and pulled up a great many bricks, and found nothing amiss; so he put down some lime and charged the master five shillings, and the smell in my box was as bad as ever. But that was not all, standing as I did on a quantity of moist straw, my feet grew unhealthy and tender. The master used to say:

"I don't know what is the matter with this horse; he goes very fumble-footed. I am sometimes afraid he will stumble."

"Yes, sir, I have noticed the same thing myself when I have exercised him."

Now the fact was that he hardly ever exercised me, and when the master was busy I often stood for days without stretching my legs at all, and yet was fed just as much as if I were at hard work.

This disordered my health, and made me heavy and dull, and often

restless and feverish. He never even gave me a meal of green meal or bran mash, which would have cooled me, for he was altogether as ignorant as he was conceited. And then, instead of exercise or change of food, I had to take medicine which, beside the nuisance of having it poured down my throat, made me feel ill and uncomfortable.

One day my feet were so tender that trotting over some fresh stones with my master on my back, I made two such serious stumbles that, as he came into the city, he stopped at the vet's, and asked him to see what was the matter with me. The man took up my feet one by one and examined them; then standing up and dusting his hands one against the other, he said:

"Your horse has got the "thrush" and badly too. His feet are very tender; it is fortunate that he has not fallen down. I wonder why your groom has not seen it before. This is the sort of thing we find in foul stables, where the litter is never properly cleared out. If you will send him here tomorrow I will attend to the hoof, and I will direct your man how to apply the liniment which I will give him."

The next day I had my feet thoroughly cleansed and stuffed with cotton, soaked in some strong lotion; and a very unpleasant business it was.

He ordered all the litter to be taken out of my box day by day, and the floor kept very clean. Then I was to have my bran mashes, a little green meal, and not so much corn, till my feet were well again. With this treatment I soon regained my spirits, but Mr. Barry was so disgusted at twice being deceived by his grooms that he determined to give up keeping a horse, and to hire one when he wanted one. I was therefore kept till my feet were quite sound and was then sold again.

Chapter XVIII
A HORSE FAIR

No doubt a horse fair is a very amusing place to those who have nothing to lose; at any rate, there is plenty to see. Long strings of young horses out of the country, fresh from the marshes; and droves of shaggy little Welsh ponies, no higher than Merrylegs, mingle with hundreds of cart horses of all sorts, some of them with their tails braided up, and tied with scarlet cord.

Then there are a good many like myself, handsome and high-bred, but fallen into the middle class through some accident or blemish, unsoundness of wind, or some other complaint. There were also some splendid animals quite in their prime and fit for anything. They were throwing out their legs and showing off their paces in high style, as they were trotted out with a leading rein, the groom running by the side.

But in the background, there were a number of poor horses, sadly broken down with hard work, with their knees knuckling over and their hind legs swinging out at every step. And there were some very dejected-looking old horses, with the underlip hanging down and the ears lying back heavily, as if there was no more pleasure in life, and no more hope. There were some so thin you might see all their ribs, and some with old sores on their backs and hips. These were sad sights to look upon, for a horse who doesn't know but

that he may come to the same fate.

There was a great deal of bargaining, of running back and forth, and there were more lies told and more trickery at that horse fair than you could imagine. I was put with two or three other strong, useful-looking horses, and a good many people came to look at us. The gentlemen always turned from me when they saw my broken knees, though the man who had me swore it was only a slip in the stall.

The first thing a prospective buyer did was to pull my mouth open, then to look at my eyes, then to feel all the way down my legs, and give me a hard feel of the skin and flesh, and then would try my paces.

It was interesting what a difference there was in the way these things were done. Some did it in a rough, offhand way, as if the horse was only a piece of wood; while others would take their hands gently over one's body, with a pat now and then, as much as to say, "By your leave."

There was one man I would have been happy to have buy me. I knew in a moment by the way he handled me that he was used to horses. He spoke gently, and his gray eyes had a kindly, cheery look to them. He offered twenty-three pounds for me; but that was refused, and he walked away. I looked after him, but he was gone, and a very hard-looking, loud-voiced man

came. I was dreadfully afraid he would buy me; but he walked off. One or
two more came who were just browsing.

Then the hard-faced man came back again and offered twenty-three pounds.
A very close bargain was being driven, for my salesman began to think he
should not get all he asked, and must come down. But just then the gray-eyed
man came back again. I could not help reaching out my head towards him.
He stroked my face kindly.

"Well, old chap," he said, "I think we should suit each other. I'll give
twenty-four for him."

"Say twenty-five and you shall have him."

"Twenty-four ten," said my friend, in a very decided tone," "and not
another sixpence - yes or no?"

"Done," said the salesman, "and you may depend upon it there's a mon-
strous amount of quality in that horse, and if you want him for cab work, he's
a bargain."

The money was paid on the spot, and my new master took my halter, and
led me out of the fair to an inn, where he had a saddle and bridle ready. He
gave me a good feed of oats and stood by while I ate it, talking to himself and
talking to me. Half an hour after, we were on our way to London, through

pleasant lanes and country roads, until we came into the great London thoroughfare, on which we traveled steadily, till in the twilight we reached the great city.

The gas lamps were already lighted; there were streets to the right, and streets to the left, and streets crossing each other for mile upon mile. I thought we should never come to the end of them. At last, in passing through one, we came to a long cabstand, where my rider called out in a cheery voice, "Good evening, Governor!"

"Hello!" cried a voice. "Have you got a good one?"

"I think so," replied my owner.

"I wish you luck with him."

"Thank you, Governor," and he rode on. We soon turned up one of the side streets, and about halfway up we turned into a narrow street, with poor-looking houses on one side, and what seemed to be coach houses on the other.

My owner pulled up at one of the houses and whistled. The door flew open, and a young woman, followed by a little girl and boy, ran out. There was a very lively greeting as my rider dismounted.

"Now then, Harry, my boy, open the gates, and mother will bring us the lantern."

The next minute they were all standing round me in a small stable yard.

"Is he gentle, father?"

"Yes, Dolly, as gentle as your own kitten. Come and pat him."

At once the little hand was patting all over my shoulder without fear. How good it felt!

"Let me get him a bran mash while you rub him down," said the mother.

"Do, Polly, it's just what he wants, and I know you've got a beautiful mash ready for me."

"Sausage dumpling and apple turnover," shouted the boy, which set them all laughing. I was led into a comfortable, clean-smelling stall, with plenty of dry straw, and after a capital supper I lay down, thinking how happy I was going to be.

Chapter XIX
A LONDON CAB HORSE

My new master's name was Jeremiah Barker, but everyone called him Jerry. Polly, his wife, was just as good a match as a man could have. She was a plump, tidy little woman, with smooth dark hair, dark eyes, and a merry little mouth. The boy, Harry, was nearly twelve years old, a tall, frank, good-tempered lad; and little Dorothy (they called her Dolly) was her mother over again, at eight years old. They were all wonderfully fond of each other; I never knew such a happy, merry family before or since.

Jerry had a cab of his own, and two horses, which he drove and attended to himself. His other horse was called Hotspur, a fine brown horse, without a white hair on him, tall, with a very handsome head; and only five years old. I gave him a friendly greeting by way of good fellowship, but did not ask him any questions.

The next morning, when I was well groomed, Polly and Dolly came into the yard to see me and make friends. Harry had been helping his father since the early morning, and had stated his opinion that I should turn out "really well." Polly brought me a slice of apple, and Dolly a piece of bread, and made as much of me as if I had been the "Black Beauty" of olden times. It was a great treat to be petted again and talked to in a gentle voice, and I let them see as well as I could that I wished to be friendly.

In the afternoon I was put on the cab. Jerry took as much pains to see if the collar and bridle fit comfortably as if he had been John Manley.

After driving through the side street we came to the large cabstand where Jerry had said "Good evening." On one side of this wide street were high houses with wonderful shop fronts, and on the other was an old church and churchyard, surrounded by iron palisades. Alongside these iron rails a number of cabs were drawn up, waiting for passengers. Bits of hay were lying about on the ground; some of the men were standing together talking; some were sitting on their boxes reading the newspaper; and one or two were feeding their horses with hay and a drink of water. We pulled up in line at the back of the last cab. Two or three men came around and began to look at me and pass their remarks. "Very good for a funeral," said one.

"Too smart-looking," said another, shaking his head in a very wise way. "You'll find out something wrong one of these fine mornings, or my name isn't Jones."

"Well," said Jerry pleasantly, "I suppose I need not find it out till it finds me out, so, I'll keep up my spirits a little longer."

A broad-faced man came up, dressed in a great gray coat with great gray capes and great white buttons, a gray hat, and a blue scarf loosely tied round his neck. His hair was gray too, but he was a jolly-looking fellow, and the other men made way for him. He looked me all over, as if he had been going to buy me; and then straightening himself up with a grunt, he said, "He's the right sort for you, Jerry. I don't care what you gave for him, he'll be worth it." Thus my character was established on the stand.

Jerry was as good a driver as I had ever known, and he took as much thought about his horses as he did about himself. He soon found out that I was willing to work and do my best, and he never laid the whip on me.

In a short time my new master and I understood each other as well as man and horse can. In the stable, too, he did all that he could for my comfort. The stalls were the old-fashioned style, too much on the slope; but he had two movable bars fixed across the back of our stalls, so that at night, and when we were resting, he just took off our halters and put up the bars, and thus we could turn about and stand whichever way we pleased, which was a great comfort.

Jerry kept us very clean, and gave us as much change of food as he could, and there was always plenty of it. And he always gave us clean, fresh water. He was kind and good, and strong. He was so good-tempered and merry that very few people could pick a quarrel with him.

He could not bear any careless waste of time; and nothing made him

angrier than to find people who were always late, wanting a cab horse to be driven hard, to make up for their idleness.

One day, two wild-looking young men came out of a tavern close by the stand, and called Jerry. "Here, cabby! Quickly, we are late. Turn on the steam. Take us to the Victoria in time for the one o'clock train. You will get a shilling extra."

"I will take you at the regular pace, gentlemen; shillings don't pay for running a horse like that."

Larry's cab was standing next to ours. He flung open the door, and said, "I'm your man, gentlemen. Take my cab, my horse will get you there all right;" and as he shut them in, with a wink towards Jerry, said, "It's against his conscience to go beyond a jog trot." Then slashing his jaded horse, he set off as hard as he could. Jerry patted me on the neck. "A shilling would not pay for that sort of thing, would it, old boy?"

Chapter XX
POOR GINGER

For a cab horse I was very well off. My driver was my owner, and it was in his interest to treat me well, and not overwork me. But there were a great many horses which belonged to large cab owners, who rented them to their drivers for so much money a day. As the horses did not belong to the drivers, the only thing they thought of was how to get their money out of them, first to pay the owner, and then to provide for their own living. A dreadful time these horses had of it.

One day, while our cab was waiting outside one of the parks, where a band was playing, a shabby old cab drove up beside ours. The horse was an old worn-out chestnut, with an ill-kept coat, and bones that showed plainly through it. Her knees knuckled over, and her forelegs were unsteady. I had been eating some hay, and the wind rolled a little lock of it her way, and the poor creature put out her long, thin neck and picked it up, and then turned round and looked about for more. There was a hopeless look in her dull eyes, and, as I was beginning to think I had seen that horse before, she looked at me and said, "Black Beauty, is that you?"

It was Ginger, but how changed! The beautifully arched and glossy neck was now straight, and lank, and fallen in. The clean, straight legs and delicate fetlocks were swelled, the joints out of shape with hard work. The face that was once so full of spirit and life was now full of suffering, and I could tell by the heaving of her sides, and her frequent cough, how bad her health was.

Our drivers were standing a little way off, so I sidled up closer to her to have a quiet talk. It was a sad tale that she had to tell.

After twelve month's rest at Earlshall, she was considered fit for work again, and was sold to a gentleman. For a little while she got on well, but after a longer gallop than usual, the old strain returned, and she was again sold. In this way she changed hands several times, always for the worse.

"And so at last," said she, "I was bought by a man who keeps a number of cabs and horses, and rents them out. When they found out my weakness, they said I was not worth what they gave for me, and that I must go into one of the low cabs until I was used up.

That is what they are doing, whipping and working me with never one thought of what I suffer; it goes all the week round, with never a Sunday rest."

I said, "You used to stand up for yourself if you were ill-used."

She said, "I did once, but it's no use. Men are strong, and if they're cruel and have no feeling, there is nothing we can do but just bear it on to the end.

I was very much troubled, and I put my nose up to hers, but I could say nothing to comfort her. I think she was pleased to see me, for she said, "You are the only friend I ever had."

Just then her driver came up, and with a tug at her mouth, backed her out of the line and drove off, leaving me very sad indeed.

A short time after this, a cart with a dead horse in it passed our cabstand. It was a chestnut horse with a long, thin neck. I saw a white streak down the forehead. I believe it was Ginger; and felt even sadder and more troubled than before.

Chapter XXI
JERRY'S NEW YEAR

Christmas and the New Year are very merry times for some people; but for cabmen and their horses it is no holiday, though it may be a harvest. There are so many parties, balls, and places of amusement open, that the work is hard and often late. Sometimes driver and horse have to wait for hours in the rain or frost, shivering with cold, while the merry people within are dancing away to the music. I wonder if the beautiful ladies ever think of the weary cabman waiting on his box, and his patient beast standing till his legs get stiff with cold.

On the evening of the New Year, we took two gentlemen to a house in West End Square. We set them down at nine o'clock and were told to come again at eleven. "But," said one of them, "as it is a dance, you may have to wait a few minutes, but don't be late."

As the clock struck eleven we were at the door, for Jerry was always punctual. The clock chimed the quarters - one, two, three, and then struck twelve, but the door did not open.

The wind had been changeable, with squalls of rain during the day, but now it came in sharp, driving sleet. It was very cold, and there was no shelter. Jerry got off his box and came and pulled one of my cloths a little more over my neck. Then he took a turn or two up and down, stamping his feet and beating his arms. But that set him off coughing; so he opened the cab door and sat at the bottom with his feet on the pavement. At half past twelve he rang the bell and asked the servant if he would be needed that night.

"Oh! yes, you'll be wanted," said the man. "You must not go;" and again Jerry sat down.

At quarter past one, the door opened, and the two gentlemen came out, got into the cab without a word, and told Jerry where to drive, nearly two miles away. My legs were numb with cold. When the men got out they never said they were sorry to have kept us waiting so long, but were angry at the charge. However, Jerry never charged more than his due, and never took less; they had to pay for the two hours and a quarter waiting, and it was hard-earned money to Jerry.

At last we got home; he could hardly speak, and his cough was dreadful. Polly asked no questions, but opened the door and held the lantern for him.

"Can't I do something?" she said.

"Yes, Polly, get the poor horse something warm, and then please boil me some oatmeal." This was said in a hoarse whisper; he could hardly get his breath, but he gave me a rubdown as usual, and even went up into the hayloft for an extra bundle of straw for my bed. Polly brought me a warm mash that made me comfortable, and then they locked the door.

It was late the next morning before anyone came, and then it was Harry. He cleaned and fed us, and swept the stalls. He was very still, and neither whistled nor sang. At noon he came again and gave us food and water. This time Dolly came with him; she was crying, and from what I could gather, Jerry was dangerously ill; the doctor said it was serious. Two days passed, and we only saw Harry, and Dolly.

On the third day, a tap came at the door of the stable, and Governor Grant came in.

"I wouldn't go to the house, my boy," he said, "but I want to know how your father is."

"He is very bad," said Harry; they call it 'bronchitis.' The doctor thinks it will turn one way or the other tonight."

"I'm very sorry to hear that," said Grant. "But while there's life there's hope, so keep up your spirits."

"If there's any rule that good men should get over these things, I am sure he will, my boy. I'll look in early tomorrow."

Early next morning he was there. "Well?" said he.

"Father is better," said Harry.

"Thank God!" said the Governor, "and now you must keep his mind easy, and that brings me to the horses. The horses will be all the better for the rest of a week or two, and you can take them a turn up and down the street to stretch their legs; but Hotspur, if he does not get to work, will soon be all up on end, and will be rather too much for you; and when he does go out, there'll be an accident."

"It is like that now," said Harry. "I have kept him short of corn, but he's so full of spirit I don't know what to do with him."

"Just so," said Grant. "Now look here, tell your mother that if she is agreeable I will come for him every day, and take him for a good spell of work, and whatever he earns, I'll bring your mother half of it, and that will help with the horse's feed. I'll come at noon and hear what she says," and without waiting for Harry's thanks, he was gone. At noon I think he saw Polly, for he and Harry came to the stable together, harnessed Hotspur, and took him out.

For a week or more he came for Hotspur, and when Harry thanked him, he laughed it off saying it was all good luck for him, for his horses were wanting a rest.

Jerry grew better steadily, but the doctor said that he must never go back to cab work again if he wished to be an old man. The children had many talks together about what father and mother could do, and how they could help to earn money.

One day, while Harry was sponging off the mud from Hotspur, Dolly came in, looking very excited.

"Who lives at Fairstowe, Harry? Mother has a letter from Fairstowe. She seemed so glad, and ran upstairs to father with it."

"Don't you know? Why, it is the name of Mrs. Fowler's place - mother's old employer, you know - the lady that father met last summer, who sent you and me five shillings each."

"Oh, Mrs. Fowler! Of course; I wonder why she's writing mother."

"Mother wrote to her last week," said Harry. "You know she told father if ever he gave up cab work she would like to know. I wonder what she says; run in and see, Dolly."

In a few minutes Dolly came dancing into the stable.

"Oh! Harry, there never was anything so beautiful. Mrs. Fowler says we are all to go and live near her. There is a cottage now empty that will just suit us, with a garden, and a henhouse, and apple trees, and everything! And her coachman is going away in the spring, and then she will want father in his place; and mother is laughing and crying by turns, and father looks so happy!"

"That's wonderful," said Harry, "and just the right thing, I should say, and it will suit father and mother both."

It was quickly settled that as soon as Jerry was well enough, they should move to the country, and that the cab and horses should be sold as soon as possible.

This was heavy news for me, for I was not young now, and could not look for any improvement in my condition. Three years of cab work, even under the best conditions, will tell on one's strength, and I felt I was not the horse that I had been.

Grant said at once that he would take Hotspur, and there were men on the stand who would have bought me; but Jerry said I should not go to cab work again with just anybody, and the Governor promised to find a place for me where I should be comfortable.

The day came for going away. Jerry had not been allowed to go out yet, and I never saw him after that New Year's Eve. Polly and the children came to bid me good-by. I wish we could take you with us," she said, and then , laying her hand on my mane, she put her face close to my neck and kissed me. Dolly was crying and kissed me too. Harry stroked me a great deal, but said nothing, only he seemed very sad, and so I was led away to my new place.

Chapter XXII
JAKES AND THE LADY

I was sold to a corn dealer and baker, whom Jerry knew, and with him he thought I should have good food and fair work. At first he was quite right, and if my master had always been on the premises, I don't think I would have ever been overloaded. But there was a foreman who was always hurrying and driving everyone, and frequently when I had quite a full load, he would order something else to be taken on. My driver, whose name was Jakes, often said it was more than I ought to take, but the foreman always overruled him.

By the time I had been there three or four months I found the work was sapping much of my strength. One day I was loaded more than usual, and part of the road was a steep uphill. I used all my strength, but could not get on, and had to continually stop. The driver started whipping me badly.

Again I started the heavy load, and struggled on a few yards. Again the whip came down, and again I struggled forward. The pain of that great cart whip was sharp, but my mind was hurt quite as much as my poor sides. To be punished and abused when I was doing my very best was so hard it took the heart out of me. A third time he was flogging me cruelly when a lady stepped quickly up to him and said in a sweet, earnest voice:

"Oh, please don't whip your good horse any more! I am sure he is doing all he can, and the road is very steep."

"If he is doing his best and it won't get this load up the hill, he must do something more than his best, ma'am," said Jakes.

"But that's a very heavy load," she said.

"Yes, it is too heavy," he said, "but that's not my fault. The foreman came just as we were starting, and put three hundred more pounds on to save him the trouble of a second trip, so I must get on with it the best I can."

He was raising the whip again, when the lady said: "Please stop, I think I can help you if you will let me."

The man laughed.

"You see," she said, "you're not giving him a fair chance. He can't use all his power with his head held back as it is with that bearing rein. If you would take it off, I'm sure he would do better - do try it," she said persuasively.

"Well," said Jakes, with a short laugh, "anything to please a lady of course. How far would you wish it down, ma'am?"

"Quite down, give him his head altogether."

The rein was taken off, and in a moment I put my head down to my very knees. What a comfort it was! Then I tossed it up and down several times to get the aching stiffness out of my neck.

"Poor fellow, that's what you wanted," she said, patting and stroking me with her gentle hand. "And now if you will speak kindly to him and lead him on, I believe he will be able to do better."

Jakes took the rein. "Come on, Blackie." I put down my head and threw my whole weight against the collar. I spared no strength, and was able to pull the load steadily up the hill. Then I stopped to take a breath.

The lady had walked along the footpath, and now came across into the road. She stroked my neck and patted me.

"You see he was quite willing when you gave him the chance. I am sure he is a fine-tempered creature, and I'm sure he has known better days. You won't put that rein on again, will you?" He was starting to hitch it on again.

"Well, ma'am, I can't deny that having his head has helped him up the hill, and I'll remember it next time, and thanks, but if he went without a bearing rein I'll be the laughing stock of the drivers. It's the fashion you see."

"It's not better," she said, "to lead a bad fashion when there's a better one to follow. A great many gentlemen do not use bearing reins now. Our carriage horses haven't worn them for fifteen years, and they work with much less fatigue than those who have them; besides," she added in a very serious voice, "we have no right to distress any of God's creatures without a very good reason. We call them animals because they can't tell us how they feel, but they do not suffer less because they have no words. But I must not detain you now. Thank you for trying my plan with your good horse, and I am sure you will continue to find it far better than the whip. Good day," and with another soft pat on my neck, she stepped across the path, and I saw her no more.

"That was a real lady," said Jakes to himself. "She spoke just as polite as if I was a gentleman, and I'll try her plan, uphill, at any rate." And I must do him the justice to say that he let my rein out several holes, and going uphill after that he always gave me my head; but the heavy loads went on. Good feed and fair rest will keep one's strength under full work, but no horse can withstand overloading, and I was getting so thoroughly worn out from this cause that a younger horse was brought in my place.

I may as well mention here what I suffered from another cause, a badly lit stable. There was only one very small window at the end, which made the stalls almost dark.

Besides the depressing effect this had on my spirits, it very much weakened my sight, and when I was suddenly brought out into the glare of daylight, it was very painful to my eyes. Several times I stumbled over the threshold, and could scarcely see where I was going.

I believe, had I stayed there very long, I would have become blind. However, I escaped without any permanent injury to my sight, and was sold to a large cab owner.

Chapter XXIII
HARD TIMES

I shall never forget my new master; he had black eyes and a hooked nose, his mouth was as full of teeth as a bulldog's, and his voice was as harsh as the grinding of cart wheels over gravel stones. His name was Nicholas Spinner.

As much as I had seen before, I never knew till now the utter misery of a cab horse's life.

Spinner had a low set of cabs and a low set of drivers. He was hard on the men, and the men were hard on the horses. In this place we had no Sunday rest, and it was in the heat of the summer.

Sometimes on a Sunday morning, a party of fast men would hire the cab for the day; four of them inside and another with the driver, and I had to take them ten or fifteen miles out into the country, and back again. Never would any of them get down to walk up a hill, be it ever so steep, or the day ever so hot - unless, indeed, the driver was afraid I should not manage it; and sometimes I was so fevered and worn that I could hardly touch my food.

How I used to long for a nice bran mash that Jerry used to give us on Saturday nights in hot weather that used to cool us down and make us so comfortable. Then we had two nights and a whole day for unbroken rest, and on Monday morning we were as fresh as young horses again. But here, there was no rest, and my driver was just as hard as his master. He had a cruel whip with something so sharp at the end that it sometimes drew blood; and he would even whip me under the belly and flip the lash out on my head. Indignities like these took the heart out of me, but I still did my best and never hung back; for, as poor Ginger said, it was no use, men are the strongest.

One day, I went on the stand at eight in the morning, and had done a good share of work, when we had to take a fare to the railway. A long train was expected in, so my driver pulled up at the back of some of the outside cabs to take the chance of a return fare. It was a very heavy train, and as all the cabs were soon engaged, ours was called for. There was a party of four - a noisy, blustering man with a lady, a little boy, a young girl, and a great deal of luggage. The lady and the boy got into the cab, and while the man ordered about the luggage, the young girl came and looked at me.

"Papa," she said, "I am sure this poor horse cannot take us and all our luggage so far, he looks so weak and worn out. Look at him."

"Oh, he's all right, miss," said the driver, "He's strong enough."

The porter, who was pulling some heavy boxes, suggested to the gentleman, as there was so much luggage, whether he would not take a second cab.

"Can your horse do it, or can't he?" said the blustering man.

"Oh, he can do it, sir. Send up the boxes, porter. He can take more," and he helped to haul up a box so heavy that I could feel the springs go down.

"Papa, papa, do take a second cab," said the young girl in a beseeching tone. I am sure we are wrong. I am sure it is very cruel."

"Nonsense, Grace, get in at once, and stop making all this fuss. A pretty thing it would be if a man had to examine every cab horse before he hired it - the man knows his own business. There, get in and hold your tongue!"

My gentle friend had to obey, and box after box was dragged up and

lodged on the top of the cab, or settled by the side of the driver. At last all was ready, and with his usual jerk at the rein, and lash of the whip, he drove out of the station.

The load was very heavy, and I had had neither food nor rest since the morning. But I did my best, as I had always done, in spite of cruelty and injustice.

I got along fairly well till we came to Ludgate Hill, but there the heavy load and my own exhaustion were too much. I was struggling to keep on, goaded by constant chucks of the rein and use of the whip, when, in a single moment - I cannot tell why - my feet slipped from under me, and I fell heavily to the ground onto my side. The suddenness and the force with which I fell seemed to beat all the breath out of my body. I lay perfectly still; indeed, I had no power to move, and I thought I was going to die. I heard a sort of confusion around me, loud angry voices, and the unloading of the luggage, but it was all like a dream. I thought I heard that sweet, pitiful voice saying, "Oh, that poor horse! It is our fault." Someone came and loosened the throat strap of my bridle, and undid the traces which kept the collar so tight upon me. Someone said, "He's dead, he'll never get up again."

Then I could hear a policeman giving orders, but I did not even open my eyes. I could only draw a gasping breath now and then. Some cold water was thrown over my head, and some cordial was poured into my mouth, and something was covered over me. I cannot tell how long I lay there, but I found my life coming back, and a kind-voiced man was patting me and encouraging me to rise. After some more cordial had been given me, and after one or two attempts, I staggered to my feet, and was gently led to a stable which was close by. Here I was put into a well-maintained stall, and some warm gruel was brought to me, which I drank thankfully.

In the evening I was sufficiently recovered to be led back to Spinner's stables, where I think they did the best for me they could. In the morning Spinner came with a vet to look at me. He examined me closely and said:

"This is a case of overwork more than disease, and if you could give him

a rest for six months he would be able to work again. But as for now, there's not an ounce of strength in him."

"Then he must go to the dogs," said Spinner. "I have no meadows to nurse sick horses in - he might get well or he might not. That sort of thing don't suit my business. My plan is to work 'em as long as they'll go, and then sell 'em for what they'll fetch."

"If he was broken-winded," said the vet, "you had better have him killed out of hand, but he is not. There is a sale of horses coming off in about ten days. If you rest him and feed him, he may pick up, and you may get more than his skin is worth, at any rate."

Upon this advice, Spinner rather unwillingly, I think, gave orders that I should be well fed and cared for, and the stable man, happily for me, carried out the orders with a much better will than his master had in giving them. Ten days of perfect rest, plenty of good oats, hay, bran mashes with boiled linseed mixed in them, did more to improve my condition than anything else could have done. Those linseed mashes were delicious, and I began to think that it might be better to live than to go to the dogs. When the twelfth day after the accident came, I was taken to the sale, a few miles out of London. I felt that any change from my present place must be an improvement, so I held up my head, and hoped for the best.

Chapter XXIV
FARMER THOROUGHGOOD AND HIS GRANDSON WILLIE

At this sale, of course, I found myself in the company of old, broken-down horses, some lame, some broken-winded and some old.

Many of the buyers and sellers looked not much better off than the poor beasts for which they were bargaining. There were poor old men trying to get a horse or pony for a few pounds that might drag about some small wood or coal cart. There were other poor men trying to sell a worn-out beast for two or three pounds, rather than have the greater loss of killing him. Some of them looked as if poverty had hardened them all over; but there were others that I would have willingly used the last of my strength in serving, poor and shabby, but kind and human, with voices that I could trust.

There was one tottering old man that took a great fancy to me, and I to him, but I was not strong enough. It was an anxious time! Coming from the better part of the fair, I noticed a man who looked like a gentleman farmer, with a young boy by his side. He had a broad back and round shoulders, a kind, ruddy face, and he wore a broad-brimmed hat. When he came up to me

111

and my companions, he stood still, and gave a look around us. I saw his eye rest on me. I still had a good mane and tail, which did something for my appearance. I pricked up my ears and looked at him.

"There's a horse, Willie, that has known better days."

"Poor old fellow!" said the boy, "Do you think, grandpapa, he was ever a carriage horse?"

"Oh yes, my boy," said the farmer, coming closer, "he might have been anything when he was young. Look at his nostrils and his ears, the shape of his neck and shoulders. There's a good deal of breeding about that horse." He put out his hand and gave me a kind pat on the neck. I put out my nose in answer to his kindness. The boy stroked my face.

"Poor old fellow. See, grandpapa, how well he understands kindness? Could you buy him and make him young again like you did with Ladybird?"

"My dear boy, I can't make all old horses young. Besides, Ladybird was not so very old; she was run down and badly used."

"Well, grandpapa, I don't believe that this one is old. Look at his mane and tail. I wish you would look into his mouth, and then you could tell; though he is very thin, his eyes are not sunk like some old horses."

The old gentleman laughed. "Bless the boy, he's as horsey as I am."

"But do look at his mouth, grandpapa, and ask the price. I am sure he would grow young in our meadows."

The man who had brought me for sale now put in his word.

"The young gentleman's a real knowing one, sir. Now the fact is, this horse is just pulled down with overwork in cabs. He's not an old one, and I heard that the vet said six months' rest would set him right up, being as how his wind was not broken. I've had the tending of him these last ten days, and a more pleasant animal I never met. It would be worth a gentleman's while to give a five-pound note for him, and let him have a chance. I'll be bound he'd be worth twenty pounds next spring."

The old gentleman laughed and the little boy looked up eagerly.

"Oh grandpapa, didn't you say the colt sold for five pounds more than

you'd expected? You wouldn't be poorer if you did buy this one."

The farmer slowly felt my legs, which were much swelled and strained. Then he looked at my mouth. "Thirteen or fourteen, I should say; just trot him out, will you?"

I arched my poor thin neck, raised my tail a little, and threw out my legs as well as I could, for they were very stiff.

"What's the lowest you'll take for him?" said the farmer as I came back.

"Five pounds, sir; that was the lowest price my master set."

"It's all speculation," said the old gentleman, shaking his head, but at the same time slowly drawing his purse, "quite a speculation! Have you any more business here?" he said, counting the sovereigns into his hand.

"No, sir, I can take him for you to the inn, if you like."

"Please do, I am going there now."

They walked forward, and I was led behind. The boy could hardly control his delight, and the old gentleman seemed to enjoy the boy's pleasure.

I had a good feed at the inn, and then was gently ridden home by a servant of my new master's, and put into a large meadow with a shed in one corner of it.

Mr. Thoroughgood, that was the name of my benefactor, gave orders that I should have hay and oats every night and morning, and the run of the meadow during the day, and "You, Willie," he said, "must keep a good eye on him. I'm putting you in charge of him."

The boy was proud of his charge, and undertook it in all seriousness. There was not a day when he did not pay me a visit, sometimes picking me out among the other horses, and giving me a bit of carrot, or something good, or sometimes standing by me while I ate my oats. He always came with kind words and caresses, and of course I grew very fond of him. I used to come to him in the field and follow him about. Sometimes he brought his grandfather, who always looked closely at my legs.

"This is our whole point, Willie," he would say. "But he is improving so steadily that I think we shall see a change for the better in the spring."

The perfect rest, the good food, the soft turf, and gentle exercise soon began to show in my condition and my spirits. I had a good constitution from my mother, and I was never strained when I was young, so I had a better chance than many horses who have been worked before they came to their full strength.

During the winter my legs improved so much that I began to feel quite young again. The spring came round, and one day in March, Mr. Thoroughgood determined that he would try me with the carriage. I was pleased, and he and Willie drove me for a few miles. My legs were not stiff now, and I did the work with perfect ease.

"He's growing young, Willie. We must give him a little gentle work now, and by midsummer he will be as good as Ladybird. He has a beautiful mouth, and good paces; they can't be better."

"Oh Grandpapa, how glad I am you bought him!"

"So am I, my boy, but he has to thank you more than me. We must now be looking out for a quiet, genteel place for him, where he will be valued."

Chapter XXV
MY LAST HOME

One day during this summer the groom cleaned and dressed me with such extraordinary care that I thought some new change must be at hand. He trimmed my fetlocks and legs, passed the tarbrush over my hoofs, and even parted my forelock. I think the harness had an extra polish. Willie seemed half anxious, half merry, as he got into the cart with his grandfather.

"If the ladies take to him," said the old gentleman, "they'll be suited and he'll be suited. We can but try."

At the distance of a mile or two from the village we came to a pretty, low house, with a lawn and shrubbery at the front and a drive up to the door. Willie rang the bell, and asked if Miss Blomefield or Miss Ellen was at home. Yes, they were. So, while Willie stayed with me, Mr. Thoroughgood went into the house.

In about ten minutes he returned, followed by three ladies; one tall, pale lady, wrapped in a white shawl, leaned on a younger lady, with dark eyes and a merry face; the other, a very stately looking person, was Miss Blomefield.

They all came and looked at me and asked questions. The younger lady, Miss Ellen - took to me very much; she said she was sure she would like me, and I had such a good face. The tall, pale lady said that she should always be nervous in riding behind a horse that had once been down, as I might come down again, and if I did, she should never get over the fright.

"You see, ladies," said Mr. Thoroughgood, "many first-rate horses have had their knees broken through the carelessness of their drivers, without any fault of their own. And what I can see of this horse, I should say, that is his case; but of course I do not wish to influence you. If you incline, you can have him on trial, and then your coachman will see what he thinks of him."

"You have always been such a good adviser to us about our horses," said the stately lady, "that your recommendation goes a long way with me, and if my sister Lavinia sees no objection, we will accept your offer of a trial, with thanks."

It was then arranged that I should be sent for the next day.

In the morning a smart-looking young man came for me. At first he looked pleased, but when he saw my knees he said, in a disappointed voice:

"I didn't think, sir, you would have recommended to the ladies a blemished horse like this one."

"Handsome is that handsome does," said my master. "You are only taking him on trial, and I am sure you will like him, young man, and if he is not as safe as any horse you have ever driven, send him back."

I was led home, placed in a comfortable stable, fed, and left to myself. The next day, when my groom was cleaning my face, he said:

"That is just like the star that Black Beauty had; he is much the same height too. I wonder where he is now."

A little further on he came to the place in my neck where I bled, and where a little knot was left in the skin. He almost started, and began to look me over carefully, talking to himself.

"White star in the forehead, one white foot on the off side, this little knot just in that place" - then looking at the middle of my back - "and as I am alive, there is that little patch of white hair that John used to call 'Beauty's threepenny bit.' It *must* be Black Beauty! Why, Beauty! Do you know me?

Joe Green that almost killed you?" And he began patting and patting me as if he were quite overjoyed.

I couldn't say that I remembered him, for now he was a fine grown young man, with a black moustache and a man's voice, but I was sure he knew me, and that he was Joe Green, and I was very glad. I put my nose up to him, and tried to say that we were friends. I never saw a man so pleased.

"Give you a fair trial! I should think so indeed! I wonder who the rascal was that broke your knees, my old Beauty! You must have been badly served somewhere. Well, well, it won't be my fault if you haven't good times of it now. I wish John Manly was here to see you."

That afternoon I was hitched to a low cart and brought to the door. Miss Ellen was going to try me, and Green went with her. I soon found that she was a good driver, and she seemed pleased with my paces. I heard Joe telling her about me, and that he was sure I was Squire Gordon's old Black Beauty.

When we returned, the other sisters came out to hear how I had behaved myself. She told them what she had just heard, and said:

"I shall certainly write Mrs. Gordon, and tell her that her favorite horse has come to us. How pleased she will be!"

I was driven every day for a week or so, and as I appeared to be quite safe, Miss Lavinia at last ventured out in the small close carriage. After this it was decided to keep me and call me by my old name of "Black Beauty."

I have now lived in this happy place a whole year. Joe is the best and kindest of grooms. My work is easy and pleasant, and I feel my strength and spirits all coming back again. Mr. Thoroughgood said to Joe the other day:

"In your place he will last till he is twenty years old - perhaps more."

Willie visits me often, and treats me as a special friend. My ladies have promised that I shall never be sold, and so I have nothing to fear; and here my story ends. My troubles are all over, and I am at home.